D1276973

Literacy Consultants
DAVID BOOTH • KATHLEEN GOULD LUNDY

Social Studies Consultant
PETER PAPPAS

A Harcourt Achieve Imprint

10801 N. Mopac Expressway
Building # 3
Austin, TX 78759
1.800.531.5015

Steck-Vaughn is a trademark of Harcourt Achieve Inc. registered in the United
States of America and/or other jurisdictions. All inquiries should be mailed to:
Paralegal Department, 6277 Sea Harbor Drive, Orlando, FL 32887.

Rubicon © 2007 Rubicon Publishing Inc.
www. rubiconpublishing.com

Project Editor: Kim Koh
Editor: Vicki Low
Art Director: Jen Harvey
Project Designer: Jan-John Rivera

7 8 9 10 11   5 4 3 2 1

Beware the Vikings
ISBN 13: 978-1-4190-3205-9
ISBN 10:   1-4190-3205-4

Printed in Singapore

PHOTO CREDITS: istockphoto: 2-5, 13, 21, 29, 37, 45-47; Indexopen: 4, 21;
The Granger Collection, New York: 21, 29, 37, 45-46

Written by
DAVID BOYD

Illustrated by
MIKE ROOTH

THORFINN

SNORRI

EGIL

FICTIONAL CHARACTERS

THORFINN THORBRANDSON, a great Viking warrior, is sent away from his village for killing a man.

SNORRI (meaning "troublesome") is Thorfinn's nine-year-old son.

EGIL, HELGI, BJARNI, ARI, and **GRIM** are warriors and loyal friends of Thorfinn. They join Thorfinn on his voyage when he is sent away.

HELGI

BJARNI

ARI

GRIM

Contents

The Vikings were fierce and warlike people who lived in the Middle Ages (500–1500). They were pirates and traders. They came from the region that is now called Scandinavia. It includes Norway, Denmark, Sweden, and Iceland.

In those days, the people of Scandinavia were called the Norse, meaning "men from the North." The Vikings were only a small group of people, but they were a powerful force.

790 ››	840 ››	860 ››	862 ››	870 ››
First Viking raids on Scotland and Ireland.	Vikings establish base at what is now Dublin in Ireland.	Vikings attack Constantinople (now Istanbul) in Turkey.	Vikings found a city in Russia now known as Novgorod.	Vikings discover Iceland and settle there.

The Vikings sailed all over Europe in their famous longships. They attacked farms, villages, and monasteries. They struck fear into the hearts of many who lived along the coastlines and riverbanks.

The Vikings often settled in the places they attacked. They lived peacefully with the local people. They had a well-organized society and strict laws.

The Vikings were also great explorers. By the end of the Middle Ages, they had sailed everywhere from North America in the west to Constantinople in the east!

NORTH AMERICA

EUROPE

Atlantic Ocean

WHAT'S THE STORY?

This story is set in an actual time in history but the characters and events are fictitious.

886 »	930 »	985 »	1000 »	1013 »
King Alfred the Great of England allows Vikings (Danes) to settle in a large part of England called the Danelaw.	The Icelandic national assembly is founded.	The Viking explorer Erik the Red discovers Greenland.	Erik the Red's son, Leif Erikson, lands in North America.	Danes conquer all of England.

VIKING LAWS

Council of elders

The Vikings kept order in their society with many laws. When a person committed a crime, he or she had to stand trial.

People accused of crimes had to prove their innocence by doing something dangerous and painful. For example, they were made to plunge an arm into a vat of boiling water or hold a red-hot piece of iron! If the hand healed, it was a sign of innocence. If it got infected, the person was guilty!

Guilty people were often punished by being declared outlaws. They no longer had protection from society. In this story, Thorfinn is declared an outlaw for murdering Olaf and is sent away.

SNORRI WAKES UP SUDDENLY. SOMETHING IS DRAGGING HIM ALONG!

WHAT'S GOING ON?

POLAR BEAR!!

HE'S TAKING ME AWAY ...

... HE'S GOING TO EAT ME! THE WAR HORN IS MY ONLY HOPE!

SNORRI'S HANDS WRAP AROUND THE WAR HORN.

HE BRINGS IT TO HIS LIPS AND BLOWS AS LOUDLY AS HE CAN.

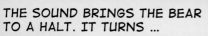

THE SOUND BRINGS THE BEAR TO A HALT. IT TURNS ...

... AND PULLS VIGOROUSLY AT THE FUR CLOAK.

LET ME GO! I DON'T WANT TO BE YOUR SUPPER!

SUDDENLY, OUT OF THE MIST, THORFINN, EGIL, AND THE OTHERS APPEAR.

THEY YELL AT THE MASSIVE POLAR BEAR.

THAT BEAR'S GOT SNORRI!

DON'T GIVE UP, SNORRI! THERE ARE SIX OF US AND ONLY ONE OF HIM!

WE'VE GOT TO HELP HIM! THE BEAR'S GOING TO KILL SNORRI!

THEY KNOW THAT ONE SWIPE OF THE BEAR'S PAW MEANS DEATH.

THE NORSE GODS

The Norse people believed in many gods and goddesses.

Odin (or Woden) was the chief god — the god of wisdom and war. He gathered all the brave men who died in battle into Valhalla — "hall of the slain" — where they feasted together in the afterlife. Wednesday (Woden's day) is named after Odin.

Thor's hamme

Thor was the son of Odin, and the god of thunder. He created thunder and lightning with his powerful hammer. He rode a battle chariot drawn by two goats. Thursday (Thor's day) is named after him.

Freya, the wife of Odin, was the goddess of love and fertility. She represented women and magic. Freya rode in a chariot pulled by two cats. Friday (Freya's day) is named after her.

Odin, god of wisdom and war

WHILE THE OTHERS SLEEP, THORFINN KEEPS HIS HAND ON THE RUDDER ...

... GUIDING THE LONGSHIP SLOWLY UNDER THE LIGHT OF THE STARS ABOVE.

HELGI SHAKES HIMSELF AWAKE AND, YAWNING, TAKES OVER FROM THORFINN.

DON'T FALL ASLEEP DURING YOUR WATCH, HELGI.

HA! I'M A WARRIOR AND I ALWAYS SLEEP WITH ONE EYE OPEN. DON'T WORRY.

IT IS QUIET AS THE MIST THICKENS AND THE MEN SLEEP ON.

THE ICEBERG IS BEHIND THEM AS THEY SAIL ON.

FIND LAND TODAY. I CAN SMELL IT.

HA! ALL I CAN SMELL AFTER TWO WEEKS IN THIS SHIP IS YOU!

ARI LOOKS INTO THE DISTANCE AS IF HE CAN ALREADY SEE IT.

LAND. A NEW HOME AND NEW ADVENTURES ...

VIKING LONGSHIPS

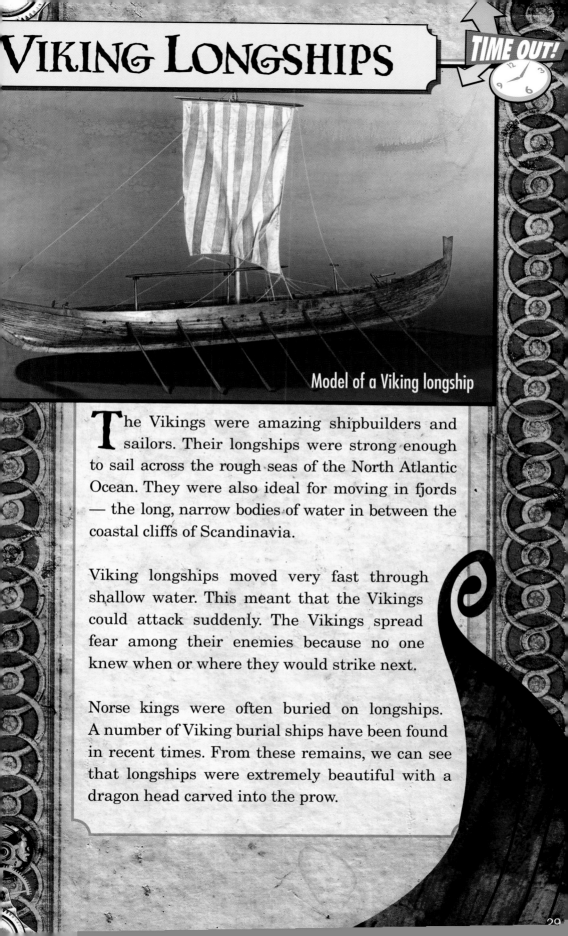

Model of a Viking longship

The Vikings were amazing shipbuilders and sailors. Their longships were strong enough to sail across the rough seas of the North Atlantic Ocean. They were also ideal for moving in fjords — the long, narrow bodies of water in between the coastal cliffs of Scandinavia.

Viking longships moved very fast through shallow water. This meant that the Vikings could attack suddenly. The Vikings spread fear among their enemies because no one knew when or where they would strike next.

Norse kings were often buried on longships. A number of Viking burial ships have been found in recent times. From these remains, we can see that longships were extremely beautiful with a dragon head carved into the prow.

SKRAELINGS, IF I'M ANY JUDGE.

SKRAELINGS? YOU MEAN THE PEOPLE WHO LIVE HERE?

SNORRI, RUN BACK TO THE SHIP AND BRING THE BUNDLE OF CLOTH THAT HELGI'S BEEN USING TO SLEEP ON.

BUT...

AFTER FALLING ASLEEP WHEN YOU WERE SUPPOSED TO BE WATCHING FOR AN ICEBERG, YOU'RE LUCKY WE DON'T GIVE YOU A STONE FOR A PILLOW.

HERE IT IS!

ALL OF YOU, TAKE SOME OF THESE PIECES OF CLOTH.

WHY DON'T WE MAKE THIS OUR NEW HOME, FATHER? EVERYTHING WE NEED IS HERE ...

AH, SNORRI. IS IT REALLY?

YES! THERE'S GOOD LAND FOR GROWING OUR VEGETABLES ...

... AND THERE IS HUNTING AND FISHING AND IT'S NOT VERY COLD ...

... NOT VERY COLD ... YET!

AND WHAT ABOUT THE SKRAELINGS?

THEY SEEMED VERY NICE.

SNORRI MIGHT BE RIGHT. PERHAPS WE SHOULD EXPLORE A LITTLE FARTHER ALONG THE COAST.

THE AIR SMELLS SWEET AND I WOULD LIKE TO SEE MORE.

HA! THEN WHY ARE WE SLEEPING ON OUR SHIP AND NOT ON THE SHORE?

THEY CONTINUE TO EXPLORE ALONG THE COAST.

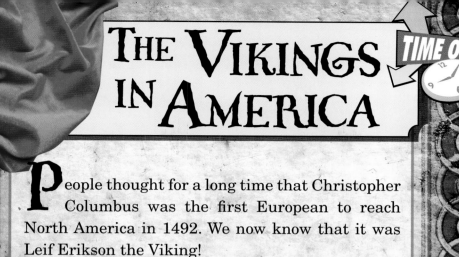

THE VIKINGS IN AMERICA

TIME OUT!

People thought for a long time that Christopher Columbus was the first European to reach North America in 1492. We now know that it was Leif Erikson the Viking!

Leif was the son of Erik the Red (named for his red hair). Erik the Red was a famous Viking explorer who discovered Greenland in 985.

Leif sailed west like his father in search of new land. In the year 1000, he discovered the places which we now know as Baffin Island, Labrador, and Newfoundland.

The adventures of Erik the Red and his son Leif were written down in the books called *The Saga of the Greenlanders* and *Erik's Saga*. For many years, scholars thought that these stories were works of fiction. But in 1960, the scholars were proven wrong ...

Norse landing in North America

YOU! YOU MADE ME LEAVE MY HOME! HAVE I NOT PAID ENOUGH? ARE YOU FOLLOWING ME TO MAKE ME SUFFER EVEN MORE?

NO, THORFINN, NO! OUR VILLAGE HAS BEEN ATTACKED. MANY OF OUR WARRIORS HAVE BEEN KILLED. YOU ARE NEEDED.

ALL OF YOU ARE NEEDED!

THORFINN, COME HOME. WE WELCOME YOU AND YOUR BRAVE MEN BACK TO OUR VILLAGE. WE WANT YOU TO BECOME OUR LEADER.

VIKINGS IN NEWFOUNDLAND

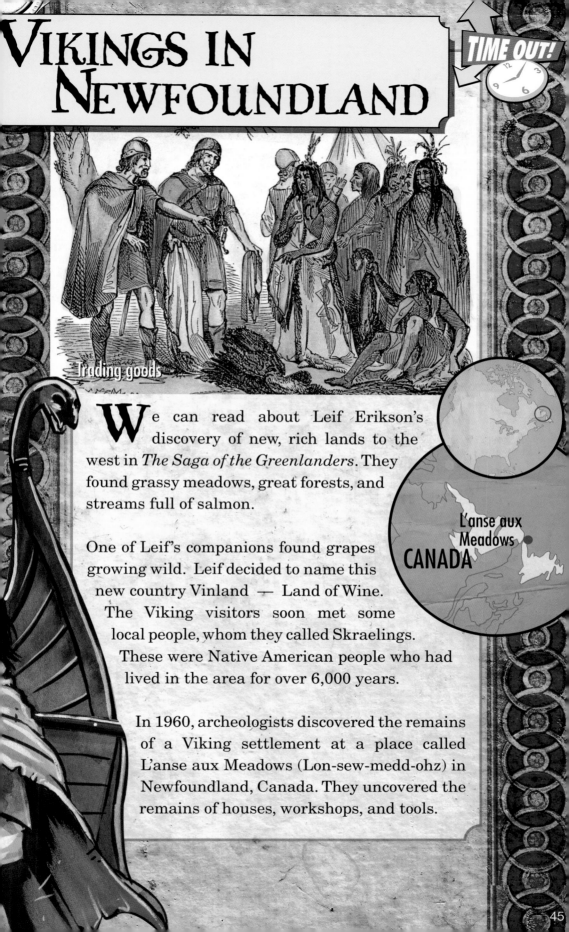

Trading goods

We can read about Leif Erikson's discovery of new, rich lands to the west in *The Saga of the Greenlanders*. They found grassy meadows, great forests, and streams full of salmon.

One of Leif's companions found grapes growing wild. Leif decided to name this new country Vinland — Land of Wine. The Viking visitors soon met some local people, whom they called Skraelings. These were Native American people who had lived in the area for over 6,000 years.

In 1960, archeologists discovered the remains of a Viking settlement at a place called L'anse aux Meadows (Lon-sew-medd-ohz) in Newfoundland, Canada. They uncovered the remains of houses, workshops, and tools.

L'anse aux Meadows

CANADA

Painting of Viking sailors

THE VIKING LEGACY

From Newfoundland to Constantinople, from Russia to Jerusalem — the Vikings went farther around the world than other Europeans before them.

Just why they traveled abroad — trading, raiding, and settling — is unclear. It could be that medieval Scandinavia was overpopulated and the Vikings went in search of land.

But the Vikings were also driven by a spirit of adventure. Their remarkable skills at building and sailing ships meant that they could easily travel farther than anyone had before — and so they did.

The Vikings are remembered for many things. Their settlement in England changed the English language forever. Basic words like "sky," "leg," and "die" are Norse in origin. The names for the days of the week — Tuesday, Wednesday, Thursday, and Friday — are all taken from the names of Norse gods.

The Norse were historians and story-tellers. They wrote about their adventures in stories called sagas. They also composed poetry about their gods and goddesses. It is from this literature that we know so much about the Vikings.